"We want water,"
they said.

ISBN: 0781438608

1

"We need water,"
they said.

"God gave us water at home,"
they said.

"Did God forget us?"
they said.

"God," said Moses.
"We need water."

"God gave us water,"
said Moses.

"Did you forget to pray?"
said Moses.

"Thank you, God!"
they said.

"No food," she said.

"No food?" he said.

"We have a drop of oil," she said.

"Go get jars," he said.

"Get lots of jars."

"We have oil," she said.
"We have lots of oil."

"We have oil," he said.
"Lots of oil."

"We have food," she said.
"God gave us lots of food."

"I spy spies,"
said Rahab.

"We are *God's* spies,"
they said.

"I spy king's men," she said.
"Hide!"

"Are spies here?"
they said.

"No spies here!"

"No spies here!"

"Thank you," said God's spies.
"You are God's spy, too."

"I am *God's* spy,"
she said.